AMAZON RIVER RESCUE

Riley,

Greetings from the Amazon, Carrot Top! I am on assignment to study the role that Kapok trees play in supporting life in the rain forest. Your Aunt Martha and Cousin Alice are here with me collecting important bark and leaf samples.

We need you to come help us out, since your endless curiosity always turns up something interesting! We all look forward to your arrival, especially Alice. She is lost without you! Don't leave me hanging,

Uncle Max

ADVENTURES OF RILEY

BY AMANDA LUMRY
& LAURA HURWITZ

EaglemonT
Press

ILLUSTRATED BY
SARAH MCINTYRE

All photographs by Amanda Lumry except:
cover background boy in canoe © Owen Franken/CORBIS;
pg. 4 toucan © Zefa Visual Media/Indexstock;
pg. 4 coati © Rod Williams/Bruce Coleman Inc.;
pg. 4 macaw © Theo Allofs/CORBIS;
pg. 4 boa constrictor © Joe McDonald/CORBIS;
pg. 4 iguana © E.R. Degginger/Bruce Coleman, Inc.;
pg. 5 tamandua anteater © Patricia Fogden/CORBIS;
pg. 9 trio of capybaras © Mary Ann McDonald/CORBIS;
pg. 14 two-toed sloth © Kevin Schafer/CORBIS;
pg. 23 jaguar © Lynne Stone/Indexstock;
pg. 25 boatmen at sunset © Alison Wright/CORBIS;
pg. 30 Ariau Towers Hotel © Ricardo Azoury/CORBIS;
pg. 31 tortoise beetle © Michael & Patricia Fogden/CORBIS

Illustrations ©2004 by Sarah McIntyre
Editing and Finished Layouts by Michael E. Penman

Digital Imaging by Embassy Graphics, Canada
Printed in China by Midas Printing International Limited
ISBN: 0-9662257-9-1

A special thank you to all the
scientists who collaborated on this project.
Your time and assistance was very
much appreciated.

A portion of the proceeds from your purchase of this licensed product supports the stated educational mission of the Smithsonian Institution -
"the increase and diffusion of knowledge." The name of the Smithsonian Institution and the sunburst logo are registered trademarks of the
Smithsonian Institution and are registered in the U.S. Patent and Trademark Office.
www.si.edu

2% of the proceeds from this book will be donated to the Wildlife Conservation Society.
http://wcs.org

A royalty of approximately 1% of the estimated retail price of this book will be received by World Wildlife Fund (WWF). The Panda Device
and WWF are registered trademarks. All rights reserved by World Wildlife Fund, Inc.
www.worldwildlife.org

First edition published 2004 by
Eaglemont Press
PMB 741
15600 NE 8th #B-1
Bellevue, WA 98008
1-877-590-9744
info@eaglemontpress.com
www.eaglemontpress.com

Library of Congress Cataloging-in-Publication Data

Lumry, Amanda.
  Amazon River rescue / by Amanda Lumry & Laura Hurwitz ; illustrated by Sarah McIntyre.– 1st ed.
      p. cm. – (Adventures of Riley)
  Summary: Nine-year-old Riley visits a rainforest in Brazil near the Amazon River while his scientist
uncle is on assignment there.
  ISBN 0-9662257-9-1 (hardcover : alk. paper)
  [1. Rain forests–Fiction. 2. Rain forest animals–Fiction. 3. Amazon River Region–Fiction.] I. Hurwitz,
Laura. II. McIntyre, Sarah, ill. III. Title.
  PZ7.L9787155Am 2004
  [Fic]–dc22
                                                                      2004005145

"I am going to the Amazon Rain Forest," Riley told his teammates. "I bet it's full of man-eating piranhas, poisonous snakes and who knows what else! Cool, huh?"

"Wow, you're lucky!" they said.

Riley couldn't wait to go, but still he wondered, *I know the Amazon is full of amazing animals, but what is so amazing about Kapok trees?*

1

AMAZON RAIN FOREST

➤ The Amazon Rain Forest is almost as big as the continental United States.

➤ If the Amazon Basin was a country, it would be the ninth largest in the world.

➤ Over 3,000 fish species are found in the Amazon River. Most of them do not exist anywhere else.

Dr. William Laurance, Staff Research Scientist, Smithsonian Tropical Research Institute

Finally, FINALLY, the big day came. After traveling for hours on a plane and then a ferry boat, Riley arrived in the Amazon. "Welcome to Brazil!" called Uncle Max. "I may have just discovered a new fungus, which I will name the Maximus Fungus."

"Wow!" said Riley.
"I'd rather have a nice animal
or flower named after me," added Alice.
"With so many undiscovered species in the
Amazon, you never know what you might find,"
said Aunt Martha. "Or what might find you!"

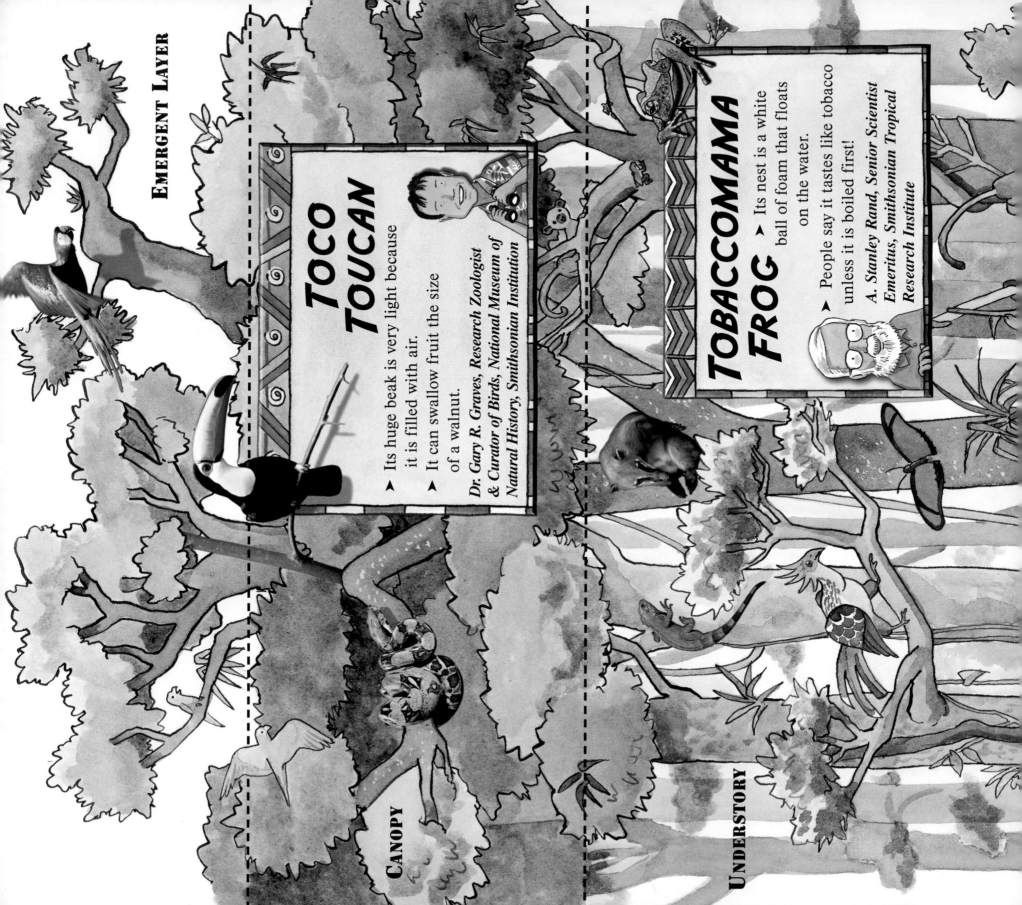

EMERGENT LAYER

CANOPY

UNDERSTORY

TOCO TOUCAN

▶ Its huge beak is very light because it is filled with air.

▶ It can swallow fruit the size of a walnut.

Dr. Gary R. Graves, Research Zoologist & Curator of Birds, National Museum of Natural History, Smithsonian Institution

TOBACCOMAMA FROG

▶ Its nest is a white ball of foam that floats on the water.

▶ People say it tastes like tobacco unless it is boiled first!

A. Stanley Rand, Senior Scientist Emeritus, Smithsonian Tropical Research Institute

LEAF CUTTER ANT

▶ Large soldier ants protect the queen.

▶ It chews leaves into pulp to fertilize fungus beds—its only source of food.

Dr. Dan Wharton, Director, Central Park Zoo, Wildlife Conservation Society

TAMANDUA ANTEATER

▶ It does not have any teeth!

▶ Its sticky tongue helps it capture ants and termites.

Dr. Kent Redford, Vice President, Conservation Strategy, Wildlife Conservation Society

FOREST FLOOR

PIRANHA

▶ It eats more than just meat—almost half of its diet is of fruits and nuts.

▶ Many more humans have eaten piranha than the other way around.

Dr. Paul Loiselle, Associate Curator, Freshwater Fish, New York Aquarium, Wildlife Conservation Society

"Why do you study trees?" asked Riley.

"Wouldn't prowling jaguars, giant alligators or even man-eating piranhas be more exciting?"

"Join me in the boat and I'll show you!" said Uncle Max. "Trees provide homes and food for animals and birds. Plus we all breathe the oxygen that trees produce. Without trees, animals and humans couldn't survive."

"Speaking of alligators, why don't we visit some caiman?" suggested Uncle Max as the sun began to set. Several sets of glowing eyes watched them closely.

This is so spooky, thought Riley.

"BOO!" yelled Alice.

"Ahhh!" Riley jumped.

CAIMAN

➤ The sex of the young is determined by the temperature of the nest before the eggs hatch.

➤ It can grow up to be 10 feet (3m) long!

➤ There are 23 different types of crocodile, alligator and caiman in the world.

Dr. Rosa Lemos de Sá, Conservation Director, World Wildlife Fund, Brazil

Riley's first night in the Amazon was a real eye-opening experience.

7

Riley and Alice got up early to play soccer.

"Riley, let's go exploring!" said Alice. Riley grabbed his backpack and hurried to catch up with her.

"Be on the lookout for tasty bugs," said Aunt Martha. "I learned how good they can be while living with a tribe in Africa!"

"Yuck!" said Alice.

At the edge of camp, Riley stopped and saw something moving in the distance.

"What are those?" asked Riley.

"Let's climb down and see!" said Alice.

"What about the sign?" Riley asked.

"Maybe they're undiscovered animals!" said Alice.

KEEP OUT

"They look like little bears!" said Alice. "I'm going to call them Alice Bears!"

"I saw them first," said Riley. "I'm calling them Rilesters."

"I think not," said Alice.

The mysterious animals jumped into the river
and began swimming away.

"We need a boat," said Riley.

"I know there is one back at camp," said Alice. "Follow me."

"Are you sure this is the right way?" asked Riley.

"Of course it is," said Alice. But, of course, it wasn't.

11

After walking in circles, they spied a red rope tied to a funny looking tree. At the end of the rope was a boat!

"Wait, don't move!" warned Riley.

Alice froze at the sight of a large, hairy tarantula. Riley scooped it up and set it on a tree branch far away.

TARANTULA

➤ The largest tarantula is the size of a dinner plate and the smallest is tinier than a grain of rice.

➤ Even though it has eight eyes, it has bad eyesight.

➤ It can live as long as 30 years!

Jonathan Coddington, Research Scientist, National Museum of Natural History, Smithsonian Institution

"Faster, Riley! I see them!"

"We'd go faster if you paddled, too," said Riley. Even with Alice's help, they could not keep up with the strange animals.

"Hey, there's a slow-moving sloth," Riley said. "I think I'll call it an Alice Sloth."

"Very funny, Riley," Alice sighed.

SLOTH

➤ Yes, it is slow, but it moves five times faster than a snail!

➤ It does everything (eat, sleep, give birth) hanging upside-down...except for pooping!

➤ It is the only greenish colored mammal. The color comes from the algae in its fur.

Dr. Michael Valqui, Mammalogist, World Wildlife Fund, Peru

"Smoke," said Alice. "I wonder
what they're cooking at camp?
I'm so hungry!"
"I think that's too much
smoke for a campfire,"
Riley said.

15

THE CAMP IS ON FIRE!

Riley's heart was pounding. They pulled the boat out of the water and scrambled up a tree to get a better view.

AMAZON RAIN FOREST

➤ The Amazon Rain Forest provides 20% of the world's oxygen.

➤ The greatest threat to the Amazon Rain Forest is deforestation.

➤ Fish and river dolphins swim among the lower tree branches after the Amazon River floods.

Dr. John Robinson,
Senior Vice President and Director
for International Conservation,
Wildlife Conservation Society

"This isn't camp," said Alice. "It's so quiet. The smoke and fire must have forced all the animals and birds away," said Riley. The wind changed, blowing a cloud of smoke in their direction. "Quick, let's get back to the boat!" coughed Alice.

19

"Alice, do you hear that?" asked Riley.
"It sounds like a helicopter."

"I don't hear anything. Wait, now I do!"
said Alice. "Do you think that's my parents? I bet
they were worried when we didn't check in at lunch!"

"Oh, no! I don't think they can see us through the smoke!" said Riley.

JAGUAR

- ➤ Yes, it can swim!
- ➤ It is the largest cat in North and South America.
- ➤ Early South American cultures worshipped them as gods.

Dr. Alan Rabinowitz,
Director,
Science and Exploration,
Wildlife Conservation Society

"This can't get any worse," groaned Alice.

"Yes, it can," breathed Riley. "Look!"

Alice gulped.

"A JAGUAR! And it can swim!"

23

They both sat very still and watched the jaguar. It paced back and forth, sniffing the smoky air before slipping into the bush.

"Whew! We were seconds away from becoming Jaguar Jerky!" said Alice.

"If we are going to get home before dark we have to come up with a plan.
Look for anything familiar," Riley said.

Nothing looked familiar to her at all. NOTHING. They paddled and paddled
around curve after curve and by tree after tree. Then she saw it!

"Hooray!" Alice yelled. "There's the red rope tied to that funny looking tree!"

"Great spotting!" said Riley.
"It's getting dark. We'll have to camp
here for the night."

"Terrific. Just what I wanted to do,
sleep under a giant Kapok tree," said Alice.

"Did you say *KAPOK*?" Riley asked.

"I have an idea. Grab your paddle!"

KAPOK TREE

➤ It can grow 10 feet in height in one year.

➤ It is the tallest tree in the Amazon Rain Forest.

➤ Its wood is used to make furniture.

➤ It is a home to many animals.

➤ Its flowers are pollinated by bats.

Maxwell Plimpton, Professor, Senior Field Biologist

"I've read about chimpanzees doing this in Africa," Riley said.

"Doing what?" Alice asked. Riley started banging on the roots of the tree, and a loud, booming sound echoed throughout the river basin.

"Doing this!" he grinned.

27

After several minutes of knock-knock-knocking, the Kapok lit up like a Christmas tree. "Who's there?" asked the tree. That voice...could it be? It was! Standing on a walkway high above them was Uncle Max, spotlight in hand, with a smile as wide as the Amazon River. "Looks like Aunt Martha was right. You never know what you'll find in the Amazon!" he said.

"We were worried sick about you!" cried Aunt Martha.
"Trees are saving our lives all the time," remarked Uncle Max, "but tonight this tree played a starring role."

"We were trying to follow a furry new animal called the Alice Bear," said Alice.

"I think you mean the *Rilester*," said Riley.

"I'm guessing it was a capybara," said Uncle Max. "That rodent is quite common around here and was discovered, and named, a long time ago I'm afraid."

"Oh," the children said sadly.

CAPYBARA

➤ Its nostrils are high on its head so it can hide under water and still breathe.

➤ It is the world's largest rodent and can weigh up to 140 pounds (65kg).

➤ Its feet are partially webbed.

Meg Symington, Director, Forests and Freshwater, World Wildlife Fund, Latin America

As they walked inside, Aunt Martha noticed a bug on Riley's shirt.

"That looks good enough to eat!" she said, reaching over to pick it up.

"Mother!" said Alice.

"Wait!" cried Uncle Max. "I've never seen an insect like this before."

"I bet it's an undiscovered bug!" Riley said. They studied it closely for several minutes, when suddenly, it flew off into the night!

"There goes the Alice Beetle!" gasped Alice.

"Don't you mean the Riley Roach?" Riley grinned. That night they all dreamed of making discoveries of their own.

INSECTS
An Amazon Field Guide

Back home at soccer practice, Riley thrilled everyone with stories of the "Riley Roach" and being lost in the Amazon. He returned to living the life of a nine-year-old...until he got another letter from his Uncle Max.

Where will Riley go next?

Further Information

Glossary

Deforestation: The process of destroying trees by burning or cutting them down.

Familiar: Well-known, often seen, common.

Fungus: Molds, mildews and mushrooms which grow without the help of the sun or true root systems.

Mammals: Warm-blooded creatures with spines, fed by milk from their mothers.

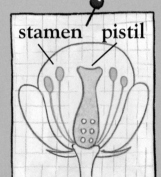

stamen   pistil

Pollinate: To take the fine dust produced in seed plants from the stamen to the pistil of the flower so that it can bloom.

Prowling: Roaming around, often in search of prey.

Rodents: Small mammals, such as mice, rats and squirrels, known for using their sharp teeth to chew.

Survive: To continue to live or exist.

SOCCER

Soccer (*futebol*) is Brazil's (and the world's!) most popular sport. The Brazilian National Team has won many World Cup titles.

Pelé, the most famous soccer player of all time, is from Brazil. Pelé first played soccer in neighborhood games called *peladas*, using rolled-up rags instead of balls.

Soccer is everywhere in Brazil! You will even find people playing soccer in clearings in the heart of the Amazon rain forest.

Illustration: Pelé and Ronaldo, popular Brazilian soccer stars.

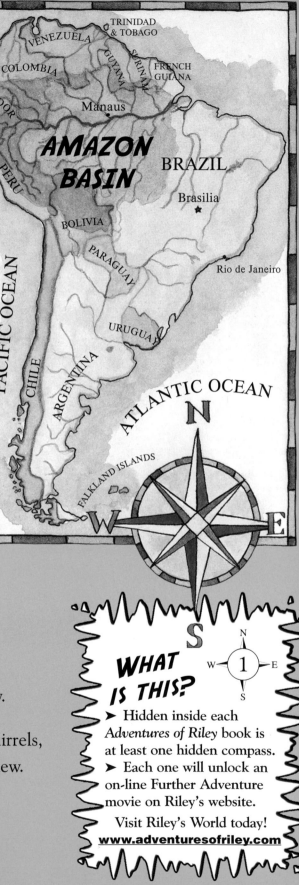

TRINIDAD & TOBAGO
VENEZUELA
COLOMBIA
GUYANA
SURINAM
FRENCH GUIANA
ECUADOR
Manaus
AMAZON BASIN
BRAZIL
PERU
Brasilia
BOLIVIA
PACIFIC OCEAN
PARAGUAY
Rio de Janeiro
CHILE
ARGENTINA
URUGUAY
ATLANTIC OCEAN
FALKLAND ISLANDS
N
W   E
S

WHAT IS THIS?

➤ Hidden inside each *Adventures of Riley* book is at least one hidden compass.
➤ Each one will unlock an on-line Further Adventure movie on Riley's website.

Visit Riley's World today!
www.adventuresofriley.com